... and Nobody Noticed the Mouse

by Enid Richemont

TOP THAT

Licensed exclusively to Top That Publishing Ltd
Tide Mill Way, Woodbridge, Suffolk, IP12 1AP, UK
www.topthatpublishing.com
Text copyright © 2013 Enid Richemont
Illustrations copyright © 2013 Tide Mill Media
All rights reserved
2 4 6 8 9 7 5 3 1
Manufactured in China

Written by Enid Richemont
Illustrated by Tiago Americo

ISBN 978-1-78244-226-4

A catalogue record for this book is available from the British Library

'For Jude and Alan, with love.'
Enid Richemont

There was going to be a
very grand wedding ...

... but nobody noticed the mouse.

Hymn Book

Flowers were brought into the very grand church – lilies and roses and tulips and ivy ...

... but nobody noticed the mouse.

The mouse scuttled
up to the organ loft ...

... but nobody noticed the mouse.

The mouse stood on one of the organ pipes ...

... but nobody noticed the mouse.

The bride and her bridesmaids came into the church ...

... and still nobody noticed the mouse.

THUD

... onto a posh lady's hat.

Then they all went off
to a grand hotel ...

... and nobody noticed the mouse.

The mouse ate his fill, then went off to sleep,
and nobody noticed the mouse ...

- TOMATO
- BANANAS

- SPAGHETTI
  CARBONARA

- LASAGNA
- TABLE ③

... except the lady
mouse who lived in the kitchen.
She **CERTAINLY** noticed the mouse!

They were married behind a big barrel of flour, where nobody noticed the mice.

And they lived happily and had lots of babies, until ...

... one day a
waitress squealed,
`MICE!'

So the mice and their babies went to live in the garden ...

... where nobody noticed the mice!